SHELBY THE Cat

To Justice,
Happy Reading!

Written By: Don M. Winn

Illustrated By: Toby Hefflin

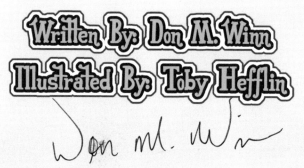

This book is dedicated to all the Shelby-like people who stay true to themselves as they stand up to peer pressure.

Shelby the Cat
ISBN: 978-0-88144-512-1
Copyright © 2010 by Don M. Winn

Published by
Yorkshire Publishing
9731 East 54th Street
Tulsa, OK 74146
www.yorkshirepublishing.com

Introduction:

When others within our own age group encourage us to do something that's either good (positive) or bad (negative) it's called peer pressure. Peer pressure can be a good thing, like being encouraged by our friends to do better in a school event.

Sometimes, though, peer pressure can be a bad thing. That's when we're pushed to do something that we may not really want to do; perhaps even something we may know is wrong. It's this kind of negative peer pressure that can be the hardest to deal with. Why is that? Because all of us want to be liked or accepted by others and if we don't go along with what the group wants to do, then we may feel left out or made fun of.

This story is about a cat named Shelby and how he dealt with bad peer pressure.

Shelby the cat
Wore a tall purple hat
And a monocle on his left eye.
He would sit in a tree
So the world he could see
And watch all the people go by.

Unlike other cats
He wouldn't chase rats,
And made friends with the birds in the tree.
He helped those in need
And books he would read,
For a renaissance cat was he.

From mice and dogs,
To squirrels and frogs,
All wanted to be Shelby's friend.
For a cat he was cool,
And not mean or cruel,
A cat on whom all could depend.

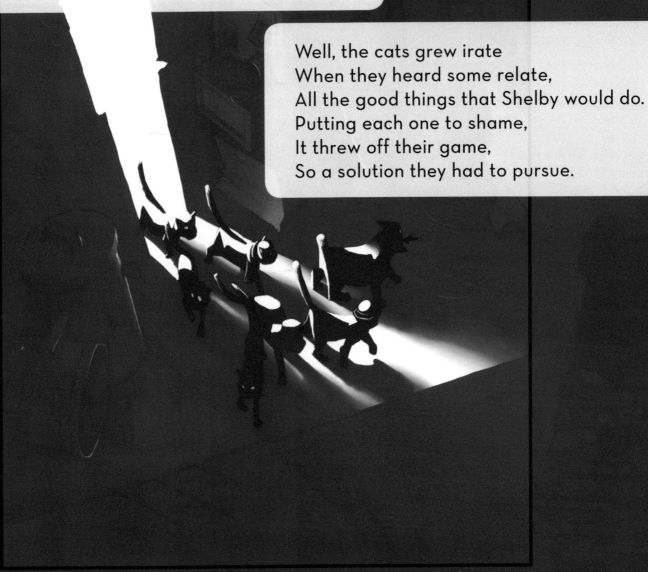

Seven cats there were
With stiff matted fur,
Eye patches and scars galore.
They would bully and cheat
Everyone they would meet,
For these cats were all bad to the core.

Well, the cats grew irate
When they heard some relate,
All the good things that Shelby would do.
Putting each one to shame,
It threw off their game,
So a solution they had to pursue.

Then the cats on the street
Decided to meet,
To discuss the Shelby dispute.
"Though cool to the rest,
To us he's a pest,
So it's time that we gave him the boot."

The cats laid in wait
Until it was late,
When Shelby went out for his walk.
"We're on to your game,
You give cats a bad name,
It's time that we all have a talk."

"You're friends with the dogs,
The birds and the frogs,
You read books and help those in need.
And never should cats
Be friends with the rats,
And cats never do a good deed."

"Decide now you must
If it's us that you trust,
And give up your friends and your deeds.
For we're all hoppin' mad,
'Cause you make us look bad,
So tell us then, how do you plead?"

Shelby already knew
What he wanted to do,
That no other course would he choose.
For right from the start
He resolved in his heart,
He would bravely stand firm, win or lose.

Shelby let out a sigh
Then gave his reply,
"You cats just haven't a clue.
You may think that you're cool,
But you're lazy and cruel,
And I'd rather choose others than you!"

It takes courage and might
To do what is right,
And not go along with the crowd.
And Shelby was ready,
For he stood calm and steady,
A cat of whom all could be proud.

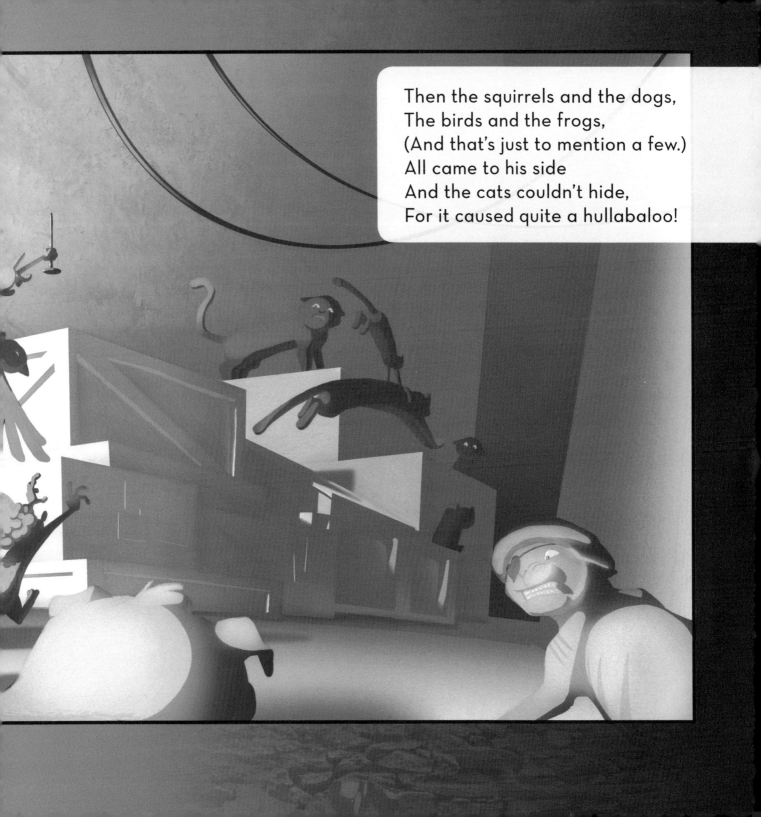

Then the squirrels and the dogs,
The birds and the frogs,
(And that's just to mention a few.)
All came to his side
And the cats couldn't hide,
For it caused quite a hullabaloo!

With egg on their face
They left in disgrace,
And would not bother Shelby again.
Shelby helped all in need
And continued to read
And daily would make a new friend.

Questions Parents Can Discuss With Their Children:

What is peer pressure?

How was Shelby different from other cats?

Why was the gang of alley cats angry with Shelby?

How did the alley cats try to pressure or bully Shelby?

How did Shelby respond to the negative peer pressure?

How can you resist negative peer pressure?

What did you learn from this story?